Topaz Publishing

READING ENTERTAINMENT FOR THE ENTIRE FAMILY

ISBN: TPEB000000028

ISBN-13: 978-0615710969

ISBN-10: 0615710964

Topaz Publishing, LLC USA

www.topazpublishingllc.com

Disclaimer: Dream Catchers is a collection of written works; authored by aspiring young artist. Every attempt has been made, within reason, to keep the child's *original* voice, flow, and meaning.

Topaz Publishing, Sr. Editor.

Dream Catchers

By

Aspiring Young Authors

Inspired by

St. Jude Children's Research Hospital

Tammy D. Thompson, Poetry

The Fall Gathering of Authors

SPECIAL ACKNOWLEDGEMENTS
"Thank You"

From the Fall Gathering of Authors

A HUGE THANKS to Topaz Publishing for publishing this book, and showing everyone what wonderful talent we have in these kids. It's a true blessing. You've given us a keepsake, one we'll always treasure.

"Thank You" to everyone who took time to read and judge these stories, including Joann Dale. She has been a huge instrument in making this contest happen year after year. You are truly appreciated.

A Note From
The Fall Gathering of Authors

Young minds journey to faraway places. Children embrace possibilities and find wonder in things adults soon forget. When you read Dream Catchers, you will gaze into the heart of a child. Using their own words, these talented youngsters have poured out their dreams, and made known, their aspirations. This collection of donated works are making a difference in the quality of life a child may experience.

During childhood, I also wrote zany poems and stories. My mother kept them inside a box, and never threw them away. Now, a mother myself, I know why. To everyone who took time to read and judge these stories, thank you. Year after year, Joann Dale has been instrumental in making this contest a success. May God bless you all. Thank you for supporting St. Jude Children's Research Hospital.

Tammy D. Thompson

The Mind of a Child
By
Tammy D. Thompson

There's a place where eagles soar
Where dreams come true each day.
There's a place where all is right
Where children are always at play.

There's a place where creatures roam
But then become your friends;
A place where fairies come to life
One that never ends.

There's a place where reality
And the dreams so dreamed come true,
A place where life turns to stories
Creating a life brand new.

This place is pure and innocent
One we all wish we could stay
This place is in the Mind of a Child
Such a special place.

For their minds expand with every
experience
And grow imaginations wild.
There's only one place like this around
It's in the Mind of a Child.

"Listen to the mustn'ts, child. Listen to the don'ts. Listen to the shouldn'ts, the impossibles, the won'ts. Listen to the never haves, then listen close to me. Anything can happen, child. Anything can be."

Shel Silverstein

TABLE OF CONTENTS

3rd Grade Stories

"Children are not things to be molded,

but are people to be unfolded."

- Jess Lair

Friendship's Helping Hand
by
Adeline L. Moss

Once upon a time, there was a girl named Lina. Lina was only nine, and youngest of the family. Roger was her brother and Rebecca was her sister. Her family was poor and got their food from their garden. Lina was in charge of weeding and watering the garden; she liked watering the flowers best! She knew every flower's kind and name.

Before Lina was born, a flower fairy worked in the garden making the flowers beautiful. This was a fact that Lina didn't know. The flower fairy's name was Tulip. Tulip loved sprinkling stardust over the flowers to help them grow. For that reason, Lina's family had the best garden in town. Their sunflowers were bigger than their house.

One morning, Lina noticed a sparkling light flying about—it was a fairy. "Hello," Lina said.

"Hello," the fairy answered. "Oh, and thanks for helping me."

Because they both loved the flowers, they became good friends. One day, Lina turned on the water hose but nothing happened. "Oh no! I've used up the water."

The fairy knew exactly how to help. "I'll give you a wish, but you must wish for water."

"A wish!" Lina was excited. "I will, I will wish for water!"

Suddenly Lina heard a poof, and the hose sprayed her face. "Thanks, Tulip!"

During harvest time, Lina met Tulip at the rose bush. She was staring at it with a long face. "What's the long face for?" Lina asked.

Tulip didn't answer; she shook her head and sighed.

Lina looked at the rose and gasped. "Oh my." Tulip had once shown Lina her fairy house. It was inside a rose—the very rose Tulip was looking at, and now, it was dead! "I'm so sorry," Lina said. "I didn't know." Tulip was her only friend, and she was felt sad.

Rebecca was bossy and fussy. She always made sure she looked good. As for Roger, he was always working in the fields. They were much too busy for Lina, so Tulip was her *only* friend.

Tulip looked at Lina sadly. "My house, my beautiful house, is gone forever."

But, Lina had an idea. "We could make you a new house!"

Tulip wiped her eyes. "We could, couldn't we. Let's start now!"

They began to work. First, Lina got some bark off a tree, then she gathered some leaves and other decoration. "Alright, let's build you a new home!"

They built a beautiful house and covered it with flowers and decoration.

When they were finished, Tulip sighed. "Best house I've ever seen. Thanks Lina!" Tulip was so tired, that she walked inside her new home and fell asleep.

Many years have passed, and Tulip still lives in the house Lina made for her. Come to my garden and see it. Maybe you'll make a new friend.

~THE END~

3rd Grade 2012

SNOW, THE CAT

by

Abigail George

A pure white cat ran through the snow. He was in hot pursuit of a car shrinking in the distance. Questions ran through his mind. Had those nice humans really just abandoned him in the freezing snow? He thought they liked him, and yet here he was, shivering in the snow. It was possible that he had done something wrong. There was really no way to tell, so he decided to leave it alone. If the humans didn't want him, then so be it. He would find another nice family, but that would have to wait. Right now, he was exhausted from following the car.

The cat woke up and felt a searing pain in the pit of his stomach. Oh, how hungry he was. He hadn't eaten in a few days. It would take too long to walk to the nearest town, so he waited for a car to drive past. A truck came speeding down the road, obviously in a hurry. The cat saw it coming and got as close to the road as he dared. As soon as he felt the wind, he jumped onto the moving truck

When the cat felt the surface of the hard truck under his paws, he shut his eyes tightly. He'd done it—he'd successfully jumped into the speeding truck. Satisfied with himself, he'd wait until they came to a town, then he'd find a new home. Slowly, he drifted off to sleep, dreaming of the perfect family.

Loud noises caused the cat to open his eyes. The city was racing by. There was no way he could jump out of the truck, it was going much too fast.

Now, the cat's dream was gone. As he watched the city growing small in the distance, he plopped down, and gave up his dream. His body couldn't move; he was too hungry, too weak, and very sad. How could he have missed his only chance for a decent life with nice people? He was so sad, that he cried himself to sleep.

This time, when the cat awoke, he noticed the truck had stopped, and there was a man standing over him. The man looked at the cat then mumbled some words. Then, he grabbed the pitiful kitty by the neck, and flung it off the truck.

The cat landed on one side. With the breath knocked out of him, his vision flickered. When two dogs popped beside him, the cat almost passed out. He was so scared; he became wide-awake within two seconds. Seeing a shed above him, he jumped a fence and climbed to the top of the shed to rest.

Someone came out of a nearby house. The cat jumped down, then leaped over the fence, taking no heed of the dogs. This was the chance he had been waiting for. He walked straight up to this person, and rubbed himself on her legs. Surely, she wanted a useful cat.

The girl leaned down and stroked the cat's white fur. "I'll call you Snow," she said.

Snow was a good name, and this would be his purrrfect home. The dogs walked up to the girl and sniffed the cat. In return, the cat held out his paw and stretched his claws on the first dog's nose. The dog whined, warning the other one not to come too close. This was Snow's new home. Maybe it was good he hadn't given up on his dream after all.

~THE END~

3rd Grade 2011

The Adventures of Buddy
And Princess
Story One

by

Aliyah Royal

Once upon a time, there was a dog named, Buddy. He was just your normal, everyday dog. There was also a cat named, Princess. She might not be your normal, everyday cat. Well, Buddy and Princess were archenemies. One blazing summer day, Buddy got a brand new throw-a-ball toy, and he was playing with it.

While Buddy was doing that, Princess was thinking. "I really don't like that dog. Maybe I should put a formula in his ball to make him fall asleep. Yeah. I heard the neighbors are moving to Alaska. I will get a box from their house and put him inside, and then he'll be gone forever!"

Princess took Buddy's ball. You know, just ripped it right out of his hands. Oh yeah, this part is where you learn if Princess is a normal, everyday cat, or not.

So, Princess took the ball and went into her lab.

"Princess!" Buddy screamed. "That wasn't very nice."

"Too bad," Princess said with a hiss. "I might give it back. I'll have to sleep on it."

"I will get you," Buddy said, as he broke through the door of her lab.

"Ah!" she screamed. "How did you break through the force field?"

"I have super strength," Buddy growled in his deep voice.

Princess smacked her face and mumbled to herself. "I shouldn't have given him that super strength drink."

"Give me back my toy," Buddy demanded.

"Nope," she said, as she kicked him out.

The next morning, Buddy found his toy. "I can't believe Princess gave back my ball. Oh well, I'll just play with it."

Buddy played with his ball for thirty minutes. Apparently, he got very tired. "Wow. I don't get tired until I play for hours, and I don't get this sleepy either."

So, Buddy went to his bed and took a nap. Soon, Princess's sleep formula put Buddy to sleep. Princess took Buddy, then put him inside the box that would take him to Alaska. But, just as Princess put him inside, he woke up, grabbed Princess, and pulled her inside with him.

"Gotcha!" he said, as they wrestled to get out. Just as they were almost out, someone closed the lid and taped the box shut.

"Great," Princess screeched, "now we're going to Alaska."

"What!" Buddy said. "We're going to Alaska? I don't even have on my winter coat." Suddenly, they felt the van moving. "What are we going to do?"

The family stopped the car, then opened the trunk of the van. "I know I heard a noise," the man said. When he opened the box, Buddy and Princess jumped out, and ran toward home.

They didn't stop running until they knew they were safe. Buddy looked at Princess. "Why do we hate each other?"

"Well," Princess answered, "when you first came to the house, everybody loved you, and forgot about me. That's why I hate you."

"I'm sorry," Buddy said. "How 'bout we be friends?"

"Ok. I forgive you," Princess said.

And they lived happily ever after. Or, did they?

~THE END~

3rd Grade 2011

Kippy the Rabbit

by

Layla Nowlin

There once was a lonely rabbit named, Kippy. The weather was starting to change, and soon a big snow was coming. Kippy needed a friend to keep him company during the long winter. Early the next morning, Kippy heard a noise outside his window. He hopped out of his burrow and saw a moving truck next door. Just as he was about to hop back inside his burrow, something caught his eye. It was a beautiful girl rabbit, and she was moving next door!

Kippy worked up his nerves to talk to her. "Hello There."

"Um, hi," said the beautiful rabbit.

"I was wondering if you would mind having dinner with me tomorrow night. I could show you around the forest."

"That sounds great!" said the stranger. "By the way, my name is Emily."

Kippy grinned. "Nice to meet you, Emily. See you tomorrow."

The next night, Kippy and Emily went to a restaurant called, Carrots and Lettuce. They had the best time ever. Kippy couldn't believe his luck. He had found the rabbit that was perfect for him.

After dessert, Kippy got down on one knee. "Emily, "he said.

"Yes, Kippy,"Emily replied.

"I was wondering if you would do me the honor of becoming my wife."

Emily blushed. "Yes, Kippy. I'll marry you."

They were married the next day. The snow had begun to set in. Together, they had four kids: Rebecca, Bobby, Rex, and Kenzy. They were a happy family.

The winter was long and hard, but the rabbit family passed the time by reading books, and telling stories. "Wait 'till you hear this one," Rex said. Rex was the humorous one of the bunch.

"I want to be next," Kenzy whined. "I never get to tell a story."

"Okay," Kippy said. "You can be next."

After story time, they all decided it was time for bed. Kippy lay down and remembered how lonely he was before he had his family. Now, he was quite happy with his life. Soon spring would be here. Life is great!

~THE END~

3rd Grade 2010

THE FIRST SNOW

by

Garrett Bennett

It was the start of Christmas break for all the children at Trice Elementary. John and his little brother, Jordan, had just come home from school, and wanted to play outside. Jordan had been thinking about how it was winter, and wished he could see snow. "John, have you ever seen snow?"

"No," said John, "but I wish I could!" The boys went on playing their games.

On Christmas Eve, Jordan asked John if he wanted to leave a note for Santa, asking him to please bring snow this year.

John replied, "Jordan, Santa might not be able to do that."

Jordan and John wrote a letter anyway, to see if Santa could bring snow.

The boys' mother called them for dinner. While eating dinner, their mom watched the news. A weather alert popped on the screen. It read, Warning: Possible snow.

Mom sighed. "Oh, that weather man is never right!"

Both boys were so excited that they didn't hear their mom. The boys hurried up and ate their dinner, so they could get ready for bed.

Once they got into bed, Jordan looked at John. "Do you think Santa will come and bring us snow?"

"I hope so!" John replied. The boys finally went to sleep. Jordan woke up to a loud noise on the roof. He slipped out of bed and ran to the window to see what it was. To his surprise, there was a white blanket covering the ground.

He was so excited that he ran and jumped on John's bed. "John, John, get up! You have to see this!" John rubbed his eyes, got up, and looked out the window. He couldn't believe it, snow!

The boys threw their shoes on and ran outside. They were so happy it snowed, that they forgot to put on their coats. They played and played till they couldn't feel their hands. Both boys ran inside to get their mom up. The boys were so excited about the snow; they forgot it was Christmas morning. This was their first snow ever. After they all played outside, they went inside to open presents.

"This is the best Christmas ever!" John said.

When Jordan opened his last present, he saw a big, glittery, red note, on the side table. It read, "Dear John and Jordan. I hope you enjoyed your gifts, especially the one outside. Love, Santa." All John could do was grin. "It really is the best Christmas ever."

~THE END~

4th Grade

Stories

Fortunately for children, the
uncertainties of the present always give
way to the enchanted possibilities of the
future.

-*Gelsey Kirkland*

Fluffy, the Fearful Bunny & his Friend, Kirby the Hamster

by

Aliyah Royal

In a lovely little pet shop, there was a hamster, named Kirby, and a bunny, named Fluffy. They were best friends. One icy winter day, it was time to eat lunch, but Fluffy wouldn't eat.

Kirby was curious. "Why won't you eat?"

"I'm not hungry," Fluffy lied.

"I know that's not true. You eat like a pig." Kirby exclaimed. "Why are you really not eating?"

"Fine. If you must know, I'm scared of carrots," Fluffy admitted.

"You're scared of carrots?" Kirby asked, quite shocked. "What happened?"

"Well, it began before I met you, when I was just a baby bunny. I was eating with my mom. She was gobbling down carrots. Then she started choking. She was coughing for almost an hour. Then she slowly stopped breathing, and passed away. I've be afraid of carrots ever since." Fluffy started crying.

"Aww. Fluffy," Kirby said. "I can't see you like this."

A ferret in a nearby cage was eavesdropping. "I remember that day. I was eating celery, but I don't remember seeing you there."

"Yeah. That's because I was really little," Fluffy said in a sarcastic voice. "I got moved to the hamster's cage because there weren't any more bunnies."

"Well," Kirby said. "I'm gonna help you overcome your fear."

"How?" Fluffy was utterly confused.

"Easy." Kirby said. "We have to make you nibble on carrots for a week. If my calculations are correct, you won't be scared of carrots anymore!"

"I hope this works." Fluffy was terrified that he'd never be able to eat carrots ever again.

The ferret chimed in. "I think it'll work."

Kirby stared at the ferret for a moment. "And who are you?"

"I'm Bob, the Ferret," he announced.

Fluffy hopped up and down with excitement. "Well, let's do it."

So, they started their plan. Every day, Kirby picked all the carrots out of his food bowl, and gave them to Fluffy. Bob was there the entire way, to motivate and encourage Fluffy. After a week of hard work, and lots of slow nibbling, Fluffy was no longer afraid of carrots!

"Thank you so much!" Fluffy said, gratefully.

"No problem!" Kirby and Bob said in unison. Now, Fluffy the Bunny is no longer afraid of carrots. And, they all lived happily ever after!

~THE END~

A FAMILY WHO CAME TO BE

by

Layla Nowlin

Once upon a time, there lived a beautiful alien girl named, Anya. She lived alone in her spacecraft. Every day, she made her own breakfast, lunch, and dinner. She even fought off other aliens that wanted her. Only today, that all changed.

A lovely, handsome, gentleman moved in down the block. He had shiny brown hair, and his skin was as green as the leaves in summer. He also had a heart as big as Jupiter. They locked eyes, and immediately, he thought the same thing about her. Then, he took the first step toward Anya, and put out his hand. The handsome man was very polite. He said, "Hi, my name is Gabriel."

"That is such a beautiful name," Anya told him. "By the way, my name is Anya."

Gabriel looked at her in a sweet way. "That is such a beautiful name, but not as beautiful as you. I do not know if you feel the same way about me, as I do about you, so please tell me. Do you like me as much as I do you?" It was silent for a while. Suddenly, the silence ended.

Anya smiled. "Yes, a million times, yes!" They both jumped for joy.

Anya and Gabriel were busy talking. They did not see an alien named, Rino behind a tree. Rino wanted Anya. "If she cares for him so much, she will sacrifice herself for him."

So, Rino and his Cyclops friend made up a plan. They heard that Anya and Gabriel were going for a walk in the woods. On that day, Rino and Cyclops waited quietly. When the lovebirds got there, Gabriel asked Anya if she would gather some firewood. Of course, she said yes, and off she went. It took a long while for her to get back. When she did, she noticed that Gabriel was gone. Anya called three times, with no response. When she called the fourth time, Rino and the evil Cyclops came out of the bushes. They were holding Gabriel hostage!

Rino said, "Come with me, or Gabriel will die!"

Anya's best friend, Lona, knew a special kind of fighting technique. Suddenly, she came around the corner. She punched them in the head, and kicked them in the stomach. After that, she tied them up against a tree. Gabriel was happy he was let go. He looked at Lona, and thanked her for her kindness. Lona just smiled. "No problem!" Anya started crying with joy.

After that day, Gabriel and Anya moved to Saturn, and had a wonderful life together. They would never forget the day they almost lost each other. No one would ever separate them, again. If you listen closely, you can hear them laughing; way, way, way, up in the sky, with their loving family. ~THE END~

4th Grade 2012

A NEW FRIEND

by
Camille Janes

A new girl named Maria had just gotten to school. Because she did not have any friends, she just smiled, and went on. She wished she was at her old school, with her old friends. How she wished she could hang out with a group of nice girls. At her old school, she had friends.

Maria headed to her first class. At least, she would be on time. On her way to class, she bumped into a tall, slender girl about her age.

"Sorry," Maria said. "I didn't mean to bump you."

"Oh. I'm so clumsy. I'm sorry, too. I'm Sally. Are you from around here? You look different."

Maria smiled and answered, "I'm from Denver."

"We're going to be late for class." Sally started walking.

Somehow, Maria thought she would meet the principal that day. They just made it to class in time. After the first class, there were more classes. It was a while until lunch.

"I didn't know we had to wait so long for lunch," said Maria.

"So how did you end up here?" Sally asked.

"Well," Maria said, "my dad is a preacher. He felt called to this town, so that's why I am here."

"Wow!" Sally said. "How long did planning take?"

"A month and a half," Maria said.

"Your dad is a preacher?"

"Yes," Maria said. "Of Beach Baptist Church, or he used to be."

"It happened fast, and it did not stop," Sally explained.

"I wish I was back home with my friends," Maria said. "What's next, after lunch?"

"Recess, of course."

Maria asked, "What are we playing for recess?"

"Tag, if that's okay with you," Sally said.

"Sure. I'd love too!"

It turned out that Sally was not the best runner at recess.

When it was time to leave, Maria was happy and sad at the same time. She would go home and relax, but she would miss Sally.

"Bye," Sally said, waving at Maria. "See you tomorrow."

"Bye," Maria said. "See you tomorrow, too." It felt good to make a new friend in a strange place.

~THE END~

4th Grade 2012

PATCH'S LESSON

by

Charli Hueter

Scout, it's so great to see you. Where have you been?" Patch urged himself to ask.

Scout gave him a very serious look. "I will not stay with you Patch. Your life is your life, my life is my life."

Patch whimpered. "But, you should help me on such a long journey. I need to find my sister, Sarah. Please don't leave!"

Scout snarled, unlike his old self. "I will leave in three days, Patch. I must teach you how to say goodbye."

Patch looked up; his eyes wet with sorrow and tears. He knew that Scout was trying to help, but to him, it was punishment.

They padded silently through the forest looking for little, lost Sarah. The next day, Patch woke under a shaded tree. It was as dry as a rock, and had claw marks, and lightning strikes all over it.

"Wow," Scout said, "that tree looks pretty powerful to be so beautiful. Doesn't it Patch?"

"Great," Patch grumbled. "He is just going to teach me another thing!" Patch mumbled to himself. Scout continued, but Patch didn't bother to listen. His mind was on finding his sister. After six miles of dreadful paw steps, they finally reached New York. It was a loud city.

They padded through crowds. Sarah's scent led them to a door. Scout was big and strong. After a few hard kicks, the door gave up and flew open. Once inside, they saw a cage sitting on a floor. Scout ran to the cage and knocked it open in one powerful blow.

"Be careful Patch!" Sarah yowled, as a Doberman with a spikey collar bowled Patch over.

Scout jumped on the Doberman. Flinging him off Patch, he sent them both into the wall. The Doberman ran off whimpering, but Scout laid still. Patch and Sarah slowly padded to Scout, their tails and heads were drooping.

Scout barked.

"Scout!" Patch yowled.

Sarah smiled at Scout with a warm look in her eyes. Patch introduced them. "Sarah, this is my friend, Scout!"

They all fell asleep with relief. The next day was grueling. After seventeen miles of harsh paw steps, they reached a sandy beach where Patch had once laid. They all collapsed onto the shore.

Patch dreamed he was falling off a cliff. As he fell off the cliff into endless water, his belly churned with fear. With each painful slam against a rock, he lost more and more hope. Finally, he flailed himself, letting the water take him. When he woke up, he realized he was dreaming; relief flooded over him

Scout gave him a very sad look. "Patch it has been three days.

"So?"

"So I must go."

Scout gave him a very serious look, but tears still glittered in his eyes. He turned calmly, and then padded off into the trees. Soon, Scout barked in the distance. "This is just to teach you how to say goodbye!" People you love are like the sunrise and sunset. They come and go, but they are never truly gone.

~THE END~

4th Grade 2012

The Lost Poodle of Paris

by

Johnni Hueter

"I hope we can make it to the Eiffel Tower by midnight." Charli ran to catch the next plane to Paris. Her sister, Johnni, tugged at the leash of their toy poodle, Sparkles. Their dream had always been to eat crepes beneath the Eiffel Tower at midnight. Now, they were on their way to Europe.

The sisters made sure they had passports, euros, plane and train tickets, and hotel reservations. After a long flight, they finally arrived at the Charles de Gaulle Airport. They then set out for a Parisian adventure. While waiting for a taxi, Sparkles slipped out of her leash and chased a cricket behind a large trunk.

Johnni looked around. "Where is Sparkles?"

They called out for their dog. "Sparkles!"

After two hours of searching, they still didn't find their little dog. Sadly, they took a taxi to the Hotel, Esmerelda.

The next day, the girls decided to search for Sparkles, again. They filled up on café au lait and croissants. "We will not have crepes until we find Sparkles. Our plan was to eat chocolate crepes under the Eiffel Tower together," Charli said, and Johnni quickly agreed.

First, the girls searched throughout the Notre Dame Cathedral. The sight of gargoyles watching them made them a little frightened. But, the beautiful 13th Century Rose Window gave them hope in finding their special lost friend. Johnni thought she saw a curly tail disappear around the Louis the XIII statue.

Meanwhile, Sparkles was also searching for the girls. She found a sausage wrapped in a crepe. She ate only the sausage, because she would not eat her first crepe without the girls. *"Where woud Johnni and Charli go,"* she thought. "The

Louvre, of course!" she barked. Sparkles saw the Mona Lisa, but no Johnni or Charli.

Remembering how Sparkles loved flowers, the girls decided to visit the Jardin du Luxembourg. There they saw a Cyclops statue, and ran through the garden. Relieved to find the pretty figure of Saint Genevieve, the girls were inspired to keep searching for their best friend. Charli thought she saw a furry paw under a geranium.

Paris was much too large to search on foot, so Johnni and Charli boarded a boat. As they rode along the River Seine, they saw the Grand Palais, the Musee du Louvre, but no Sparkles.

"Friends keep promises," Charli said.

"Yes. We promised to be under the Eiffel Tower at midnight," exclaimed Johnni. "It's eleven thirty, now," they shouted. "We need to hurry to the tower!"

By this time, Sparkles decided to go to the Eiffel Tower, too. The smell of crepes directed her nose right under the Eiffel Tower. The girls smelled the crepes, too, and followed their noses. They couldn't believe their eyes when they saw Sparkles. The clocked chimed twelve times as the three friends celebrated under the Eiffel Tower. Together they enjoyed chocolate crepes, and friendship. "Friends never give up on each other."

~THE END~

4th Grade 2012

Tiger

My Best Friend

by

Judah 'Zack' Franklin

My best friend was my favorite cat. He died a few months ago. That's why I wrote this story, or should I say, this poem. My cat was brave, smart, and also caring. When he saw a mouse, he wouldn't stop staring.

He was gray, black, and striped all over. He had more than nine lives. He was lucky as a clover. He was really a family member, more than a cat. When it was time for dinner, guess where he sat?

He ate with us, slept with us, played with us too. Whenever I was sad, he knew just what to do. Yes, Tiger was my buddy, my very best friend. I thought we'd be together to the very, very end.

We dreamed of growing up and conquering the world. I dreamed of what I'd do; he dreamed of catching squirrels. I talked about being a Pro athlete, and in the hall of fame. I'd say, "I wish you could talk." He looked as if he wished the same.

My cat was so adorable with his chin colored white. He had stripes on his gray fur, just as dark as night. He ran so fast and jumped so high. He could cry so loud it hurt. He'd spend hours getting himself clean after rolling in the dirt.

One sad Monday, after I returned from school, I called him and called once more. He didn't come running like he usually did, or pounce as I walked through the door. I looked all around, high and low, then found him by my feet. My best friend Tiger, was lying peacefully at the edge of the quiet street.

I've never been so sad as then, or cried so many tears. My best friend was gone. He'd been there for me, many happy years. I miss Tiger each and every day. I hate that we are apart. But, I know Tiger's safe; he's in a happy place, and forever in my heart.

~THE END~

4th Grade 2012

THE NEW BUNNY

by

Kayla Shew

One morning, a bunny named Taylor got up, got ready for school; then she was off. On the schoolyard, Taylor saw her friend Elizabeth.

"Elizabeth!" she yelled

Elizabeth stopped so she could hop up to her. "Oh, hey."

"I heard we're getting a new bunny in our class."

Taylor rolled her eyes. "Oh, great. What's her name?"

"Makenzie."

"Oh. That's a pretty name."

"So, when's she coming to class?" Taylor asked.

"Today." Elizabeth answered.

They went inside their school, then went to their classroom. There they saw

Makenzie. No one talked to her. Because no one would be her friend, they went along with everybody else, and didn't talk to her either.

After doing their work, it was lunchtime. They got their trays and sat down at their normal table. Taylor saw Makenzie sitting at a table alone, so she got up and sat with her. When Elizabeth saw Taylor was gone, she got up, and went to the table with Taylor and Makenzie. Now, Makenzie had two new friends. Then, all of Elizabeth's friends came over to the table, too. By the end of the day, Makenzie had a lot of new friends.

~THE END~

4th Grade 2012

Siobhan & the Enchanted Forest

When you help someone, it benefits you as well.

by

Shay N. Gibson

Once, a girl lived in a small house on the edge of a forest, in Ireland. Her name was Siobhan. Every year, on her birthday, she would walk through the forest, but this year was different. This year, she would turn 19, which meant she had to go into the forest alone. She wished her mum would come too.

It was time for her walk, so she grabbed her stuff, and started off. After a while, Siobhan stopped to rest. She saw something that scared her half to death; it was a unicorn, a fairy, and a leprechaun, and they asked for her help. Siobhan wasn't sure at first, but finally she said, "Yes!"

As they led her to where they lived, she saw a field with a house in the middle. Siobhan asked, "Who lives there?"

The creatures said, "It's the most handsome 19 year old boy, and his Mum and Dad. We promise that if you help us, he will love you. You will get married, and then have three handsome boys, three beautiful girls, and a dog."

"What do you need help with?" asked, the young woman.

The leprechaun said, "People have been stealing my gold."

"People are cutting down my trees," said the unicorn.

"People are eating my fruit," said the fairy.

Siobhan thought and thought, then she came up with a great idea. She was going to turn the forest into a protected park. Within the month, she made benches, picnic tables, planted a garden, and dug a pond. When she had finished, it was the most beautiful place in the whole world.

Siobhan had saved her friends. Then, she and the boy met for the first time. It was love at first sight, and two or three years later, she had triplets; they were girls. A year later, she had three boys, just as the creatures had promised. And, they never worried about people, again. Siobhan would go into the park each year, on her birthday.

~THE END~

Sarah Clara

The Giving Pumpkin

by

Bailey Paschal

Two twins named Sarah and Clara, lived in a beautiful farmhouse. One crisp, fall, Saturday, the girls woke up.

"Get up and get ready!" Sarah said.

"Roger that," Clara agreed.

The two girls got dressed and ran down the stairs. They each grabbed a piece of bacon, and then drank some orange juice. After putting on their sweaters, they ran outside.

"Race you to the pumpkin patch." Clara rushed out the door.

Sarah chased her sister out the door. "You're on!"

The girls had waited all week to see their biggest pumpkin in the pumpkin patch. It was as big as an oven. When the girls got to the pumpkin, they looked at it proudly.

Clara gasped. "This thing is huge."

"I bet it weighs a ton." Sarah smiled and ran her hands along the outside of the huge pumpkin.

"We definitely can't carry it to our house and we can't roll it either, or it might break," Clara said.

"Let's use a wheelbarrow," Sarah exclaimed.

Clara stared at her. "But you said we couldn't carry it."

"Yeah, but Dad can help us lift it."

Clara looked back toward the house. "Do you want me to get him?"

"Sure and I can get the wheelbarrow," Sarah said.

"I will be right back." Clara headed to search for their dad.

Clara found her dad in the apple orchard, picking apples to make apple pie for the fall festival. Clara told her dad she needed some help lifting their pumpkin

Meanwhile, Sarah was already back at the pumpkin patch with the wheelbarrow. "Finally." She sighed. "Dad, can you help us lift this pumpkin in the wheelbarrow?"

"Sure," her Dad said.

They put their hands under the pumpkin, and they lifted with all their might. Then they put the pumpkin in the wheelbarrow with a small thud. Afterwards, all three pushed the wheelbarrow to the field.

"Do you need anything else?" Dad asked.

"Yeah," Sarah and Clara said at the same time. "Could you carve the pumpkin so we can enter it into the Fall Festival?"

"I can do that, but then I have to pick my apples for the festival." Dad smiled.

Sarah and Clara's mom came outside and shouted, "You girls need to come inside, and get your hot chocolate."

The next morning, Clara awakened to the sound of a truck's engine. She got up and looked out of her bedroom window. It was the mail truck. Then, she woke Sarah up so they could go and check the mail. They got up, got ready for the day, and tiptoed down the stairs.

When they went outside, they ran to their mailbox. Sarah opened it, and found a giant yellow envelope. On the front, it said, "Help us!" Sarah opened it. She read: "Dear reader. We would like you to volunteer to gather up as much money, toys and candy as you can. Then bring it to our new festival called, 'The Giving Pumpkin'. Fill your jack-o-lantern with treats for the homeless children who cannot afford Halloween treats.

"Come look at this Clara," Sarah shouted.

Clara came over and looked at the letter. Her smile faded. A look of disappointment spread across Clara's face. "But I thought we would enter our jack-o-lantern in the fall festival."

"I know. We were going to enter it, but these kids need this stuff more than we do," Sarah said.

Suddenly, Clara's smile came back. "I guess we can afford to get costumes, and buy candy for Halloween," Clara said.

"Besides," Sarah said, "It would be fun to see the smiles on the kids' faces when we give them their Halloween treats."

Sarah put the letter in her pocket, and they both ran inside to show their mom and dad.

"Look." Sarah gave the letter to her mom and dad. "Read this letter." Then, Sarah and Clara told them their plan.

Mom and dad smiled. "That would be a wonderful and generous idea."

After their mom and dad got dressed, they all went to the store and bought lots of delicious candy. Then, they bought lots of nice toys.

They went back home, and counted all their money. Sarah and Clara made money donations, too. After their dad finished carving the pumpkin, they filled it with all the treats and lifted the pumpkin into the back of the pickup truck.

Sarah and Clara's mom looked at the address, and followed the directions to where they were going. When they pulled in, they saw a building with an alley. In the alley, they saw lots of people, and lots of jack-o-lanterns filled with treats.

"This must be it," Clara said.

So, they lifted their pumpkin out of the pick-up truck and carried it all the way to the alley. They put it down on the ground. A lady walked up to them and said, "Thank you! Please come and meet the family who will get all of these treats."

She led Sarah, Clara, and their parents to the middle of the alley. There they saw some skinny people who wore old clothes. There were two small children, and their parents.

"Hi," Sarah and Clara said.

"Hi," replied the two small kids.

Sarah and Clara's dad brought the pumpkin to the poor family. The two skinny kids screamed with excitement.

"Congratulations," the lady said. "You have the biggest pumpkin of our whole entire festival. You get the 1st place ribbon. You also get 100 free tickets for the rides in the Fall Festival."

"Thank you," Sarah and Clara said at the same time.

The poor family said, "Thank you so much for all you have done!"

Sarah and Clara went to the Fall Festival. They were all smiles, especially Sarah and Clara. They knew they had just done something very generous. It was cold and frosty outside at the Fall Festival, but Sarah and Clara's hearts felt very warm and generous. During the time they were at the festival, they had smiles on their faces. It was the best day of their entire lives.

~THE END~

4th Grade 2011

Jack and the Baby Husky

by

Kasey Whittington

Once there lived a little boy named, Jack. One day, in the cold, cold, winter, Jack decided he was going to build a snowman. Jack put on his hat, gloves, jacket, and boots, and then he went outside. Jack was rolling the bottom of the snowman when he heard something rustling in the bushes. Jack stopped, but then, he ignored the sound.

Jack started to roll the middle of the snowman. He heard the sound again, so he stopped what he was doing, ran inside, and locked the door. It started to get dark outside, and Jack decided he would go to sleep early. When Jack woke up the next morning, he thought to himself, *"I did not hear any noise last night, so I guess I was just exaggerating."*

After Jack ate his breakfast, he looked outside to see if his snowman was still up; luckily, it was. So, Jack went outside and started to roll the top of his snowman. Suddenly, he heard the same noise again. This time, Jack stayed calm and kept doing what he was doing. When Jack finally finished his snowman, he heard a voice. Jack looked all around, but he could not see anything.

Then, a little voice said, "Down here."

Jack looked down and saw a baby husky. He was terrified. "Did you just say something?"

The baby husky said, "My family and I were supposed to move yesterday, but I got lost."

Jack told the baby husky that he would help him find his way back. It was getting late outside, so Jack and the baby husky went inside to eat supper. After they ate, Jack and the baby husky went to bed.

The next morning they woke up. Jack put on his clothes, and then he and the baby husky went to look for the baby husky's home. Jack and the baby husky searched for hours and hours. Still they could not find the baby husky's home.

Soon, they started to get hungry. Jack said, "How about we go back home for lunch?"

When they arrived home, Jack stopped to scrape the snow off his shoes. While he was doing that, the baby husky started to look sad. Jack told the husky not to get upset, and they went inside to eat lunch. After lunch, they went back out to look for the baby husky's home. Jack was worried that they would never find husky's home.

They looked for hours, and still could not find baby husky's home. Soon, Jack and the baby husky got tired. It was three o'clock, so they went home. When Jack and the baby husky got home, they sat on the couch and watched T.V.

After a few hours, Jack and the baby husky went back out to look for baby husky's home. They looked and looked, but they did not find the baby husky's home. It was starting to get dark outside so the baby husky and Jack went home. They watched T.V. for about two hours, and then they went to bed. The next morning, they went back out to look, again.

They looked as hard as they could, and they still did not find baby husky's home.

They decided they would go back home and rest. While they were watching T.V., The baby husky started to cry. Jack told the baby husky that he did not need to cry.

The baby husky said, "I will never find my home."

Jack stared at the baby husky and said, "We are not looking for your home anymore, because you are at home."

The baby husky stopped crying and jumped with joy. Jack and the baby husky played with each other every day. They always loved each other.

~THE END~

4th Grade 2010

The Four Squints

by

Rachel Nadeau

My name is Rachel N., and this is my story. I believe I am the original squint. My friends may disagree with that since we all have the same strange habit. Currently, there are four of us, and we are famously known as the Four Squints. This secret alliance has lasted for four years, and we hope it will last forever.

Our adventure began way back in kindergarten, which seems like forever. There were only three squints back then; me, Morgan, and Rachel J. Our adventure began on the first day of school, as we were all playing on the playground. As we wandered around by ourselves, squinting at the sky, we somehow managed to collide into each other. When we bumped into each other, we all laughed and apologized for not watching where we were going.

I asked, "What are ya'll squinting at? Again, we all laughed. We realized that we liked looking at the sky and trees through squinted eyes.

Rachel J. said, "I like the way it makes everything look, and the way it kinda makes me dizzy."

We all agreed, and with eyes squinted, we shook hands and began to play. From that day forward, we became known as the Three Squints.

That day, just as we became friends, the recess bell sounded and we had to return to class. We were all in the same class, and that made us very happy. Now, we could play together every day.

Each day we examined things, and played all kinds of squinting games. Everyone wanted to know what we were up to, because we mad up our games. We kept that a secret, because on that first day, long ago, we made an oath; our squinting game would remain our special, little secret.

Each year, we continued to play our squinting games, and we continued to make others curious. In the third grade, we began to get bored with our squinting games, but we continued to be best friends. One day, on the playground, we were squinting at Pago, our unofficial bodyguard. We noticed someone new, walking around by herself; squinting at the sky. We began to laugh hysterically; we knew we had found our fourth squint.

We ran up to the squinting girl and said, "What's your name, and what are you squinting at?"

She looked at us strangely and said, "My name is Elsie, and I'm squinting because I have lost my glasses!"

Again, we laughed, and told her we would help find them. So, arm in arm, with eyes squinted, we looked for Elsie's glasses. As we walked around squinting, looking for her glasses, Elsie wanted to know if we were making fun of her.

"No way!" we exclaimed! We have been squinting since we first met in kindergarten. We would like you to become our first, new, official member. We have lots to tell you.

~THE END~

Bella's Best Day Ever

by

Elaina Robertson

Once upon a time, there was a dog-named Bella Kelly. Summer is her favorite time of the year. Bella has blue eyes like the ocean. She is white like the new fallen snow in the winter, and her ears are as floppy as an Easter Bunny's.

Well, one day Bella was very bored. She asked her mom if she could go to the park. Her mom said, "You may go, but only for 3 hours, we have to eat lunch."

So, Bella ran to the park. When she got to the park, she went up the stairs to the playground, then she went to the slides. Bella couldn't decide whether to go on the bump slide, the swirly slide, or the straight slide first. She asked a girl some questions about herself, and the slides.

The other dog said, "My name is Scarrlet, and I'm a dog, like you. I like dog bones, shoes, balls, and I like to play Frisbee."

Bella said, "Me too."

Scarrlet and Bell played together for two hours. Bella was having so much fun with Scarrlet, that she forgot all about the slides.

An hour later, Bella said she had to go home to eat lunch, but then, Bella had an idea. She asked Scarrlet if she was hungry.

Scarrlet said, "Yes. I'm so hungry I think my stomach is going to eat itself."

So, Bella took out her phone and called her mom. She asked her mother if she could bring a friend over for lunch. Her mom said yes. Bella said "Come on Scarrlet, we have got to eat before we starve to death."

The two friends ran to Bella's house. When they got to her house, Bella's mom, Rachel, had cooked her famous spaghetti tacos. Spaghetti tacos were Bella's favorite food. Scarrlet had never heard of spaghetti tacos, so she said she wanted a little taco.

Rachel gave her what she wanted to eat. When Scarrlet took her first bite, she was addicted to Rachel's food. By the time she was done, she had eaten five spaghetti tacos. Scarrlet said, "I'm going to pop like a balloon."

Bella and her mom ate three spaghetti tacos. Their jaws dropped, they were so amazed. Scarrlet must have eaten too many tacos, because her stomach started to roar like a lion. She went in the living room to lie on the couch.

Then, Bella went in the living room with Scarrlet. Scarrlet said her stomach felt better, so they went outside.

Bella had a big back yard, so Scarrlet asked her if she wanted to race around the yard. Bella said, "Sure."

Rachel came outside to watch them play. "On your mark, get set, go!" she said.

Bella and Scarrlet ran as fast as they could. Bella tripped, so Scarrlet won. Then, it was time for Scarrlet to leave. Rachel called Scarrlet's mom and she went home. That is Bella's Best Day Ever!

~THE END~

5th Grade

Stories

"We call a child's mind *small* simply by habit; perhaps it is larger than ours is, for it can take in almost anything without effort"

-Christopher Morley

5th Grade 2012

THE JOURNEY WEST

by

Justin Chaffin

There once was a boy named Bud, who lived in a foster home. He lived there because his mother and father had died. His foster parents were mean, and had a twelve-year-old son named Todd. Todd loved to fight all the time. At times, Bud wished he had a real brother. Bud woke up one morning and Todd was hitting him.

Bud built up enough courage to swing back at him. Todd knocked Bud off the bed, and Bud swung at him again. This time, he hit him. The foster mom came into the room. Todd started holding his neck like a big animal was trying to come out of him.

"How could you, Bud?" she said angrily.

Bud climbed under the covers so she couldn't see him. His foster mom told him to apologize to Todd, and he did. When she was shutting his bedroom door, Bud could see Todd smiling at him.

Bud's foster mom put Bud out in the shed with a blanket and pillow, so he went to sleep for a little while, and then he woke up. He thought he saw a bat, then grabbed a rake and swung. Instead, it was a hornet's nest.

There was a small window, barely open, just big enough for him to crawl through. He got out and rolled around on the ground, until the hornets left him alone. Then, Bud went back inside the house, picked up their shotgun. He put it in a corner on the back porch where they couldn't find it, then he grabbed a suitcase he had already packed, and then he left.

Bud went to the train station and jumped on the train when no one was looking. He ended up in California, and by the time he arrived, he was very hungry.

When he got off the train, he noticed a nice lady. She said her name was Ms. Hill, a librarian.

"What are you doing here?" she asked.

"I'm looking for a home," Bud said.

She paused, and then said, "Let's see. I need to make arrangements, but you can stay with me."

They went to her house. She was really nice to Bud. Bud said, "Thank you, for giving me a place to stay."

She smiled and said, "Everybody needs a home."

Bud finally found what he was looking for. ~THE END~

The Fairy Necklace

by

Maelyn Moss

One warm, spring day, a young fairy came flitting through the trees. She stopped for a moment to get her bearings when she thought she heard someone crying. She flew near the sound, but what she saw made her stop very suddenly.

There, sitting on a log, was a young human.

The fairy flew onto the log and sat down beside the little girl. "Why are you crying?" the fairy asked.

"I'm crying because I don't have a family, and nobody will take me in!" said the little girl.

"I'll take you in. And, by the way, my name is Mary Ann."

"It's nice to meet you. My name is Susan."

Mary Ann placed a necklace around Susan's neck, and smiled. "Here, take my hand, and hold on tight!"

Susan held her hand very tight. Suddenly she felt happier, excited, and older. There was a flash of light, then she saw trees, flowers, waterfalls, and more fairies. There were big fairies and little fairies; thousands, upon thousands, of fairies.

Finally, Mary Ann said, "Here we are!"

Susan found herself in a huge room, and at the other end of the room there was a glorious throne, and sitting on that throne, was a beautiful fairy queen.

"Hello, Mary Ann," the queen said. "How may I help you?"

"Well, I was wondering if you could give Susan here, a home."

"Of course I can. I will start looking right now." With that, the queen flew off her throne, and then flew away.

"Come on," Mary Ann said, "let's go play in the water falls."

Later, when Susan was asleep, Mary Ann flew back to the palace. She flew through the window and into the library where the queen was waiting.

"Are you ready?" the queen asked.

"No," Mary Ann said.

"Why not?" the queen asked.

"I don't want her to leave!"

"I know you don't want her to leave," the queen said, "but she will be happier in her own world."

Mary Ann sighed. "I'm ready now."

So, Mary Ann and the queen went back to her house. They went into Mary Ann's room and stood on either side of the bed where Susan slept. The queen began to chant some strange words, and Susan's figure started to glimmer and fade. All of a sudden, Susan disappeared.

When Susan woke up, she wasn't in Fairyland anymore. She was in her own world. Then, she looked around the room. The bed she was lying in was rather small, with a huge, pretty quilt on it. The bed was in a small room, and sunshine streamed through the window.

Susan wondered, *"Was Fairyland all a dream?"* She felt her neck. There she found the cool, smooth, figure of the fairy necklace, Mary Ann had given her. It was still there, so it wasn't a dream.

~THE END~

5th Grade 2011

Story

by

Brianna Hall

"Staci," Mira texted.

"I'm sorry, it just slipped out," Staci texted back.

Staci and Mira texted on their phones while they walked separately to school. The warm summer wind brushed against Mira's cheek. It was the end of summer, and the fifth week of school, and Staci had spilled the beans about Mira liking Brad.

Bling, bling. Mira's phone vibrated in her hands. It was Staci. It said, *"I'm sorry, are you mad?"*

Mira was annoyed by the message. *Bling, bling.* It was her phone, again, and it was Staci. Mira read the message. *"Are you still my friend?"* After twenty minutes of being mad, Mira finally sent a message back.

Staci's phone vibrated in the back pocket of her Justice jeans. She quickly took the phone out of her back pocket and read the short text. It said, *"It's okay, you are still my friend."*

Staci thought, *"I feel so bad. I'm so glad she still wants to be my best friend. I have got to remember to keep secrets."*

Those exact words were in Staci's head all day long. In East lab, she'd felt so bad about telling Brad, that Mira liked him, she deleted her folder by accident. In gym, she got hit on the head with the volleyball four times.

All day long, Mira and Staci both felt bad. Mira felt bad for being mean, and overreacting. Staci felt bad that she'd told Brad, Mira liked him. Mira and Staci walked outside with the other fifth graders. When they saw each other, and in the heat of the moment, they finally hugged.

~THE END~

5th Grade 2010

Madison and Blaire Enjoy Summer With Imagination?

by

Blaire Berry

Madison and Blaire live in Lotsville, Ville. Today is the first day of summer, their favorite season, and they're ready to make a splash.

"Are you ready?" Madison asked.

"You know it," Blaire said, with a smile on her face.

"Let's go!" they shouted.

Off they went to the public pool, a few minutes away. When they got there, it was crowded. Apparently, everyone else was thinking the same thing.

"What are we going to do, now?" Madison asked.

"I don't know. It sure is crowded."

"Let's go back home. Maybe we can come again, later.

They walked home, regretting even going to the pool.

"I still don't know what to do," Madison said.

Blaire thought for a minute and suddenly gathered up an idea. "I've got it!" Blaire shouted.

What?" Madison looked up, surprised.

"We don't need a pool to actually have a pool. We can have a pool in our minds."

"What?" Madison did not understand this at all. "So you mean, I'll have to hop into my head?" Madison asked, confused.

"No. I mean, we can imagine a pool, with the diving boards and all that stuff." "I don't know." Madison looked doubtful.

"Oh, come on, just try it," Blaire urged Madison.

"Have you done it before?" Madison asked. "No, but it's worth a try. Besides, if you clear your mind of everything for a while, you'll be there," responded Blaire.

"All right, but let's make some snacks before we take a journey to imagination land." Madison hopped off the bed and headed for the kitchen.

"Okay. I'll make smoothies, and you make some Popsicles."

"Whatever." Madison rolled her eyes.

They made the smoothies, and then put the juice in the freezer to make Popsicles.

"Okay," Blaire said. "Take my hand. Now, close your eyes, and clear your mind of everything until nothing exists. Now, open your eyes," Blaire said. When they opened their eyes, the whole house had disappeared. There was a big blue pool with a waterfall where the house had been. The snacks they made were on a table to the far left.

"Whoa!" Madison shouted in surprise. "I didn't think it was possible!"

"Cannon ball!" Blaire shouted and jumped into the pool.

Madison followed. They had a great time racing, and playing Marco Polo in the pool. A few dives into the pool ended the day, but started the summer. This was the best day of their lives, and all because they used their imagination.

~THE END~

6th Grade

Stories

"Your imagination is your preview of life's coming attractions."

~Albert Einstein

6th Grade 2012

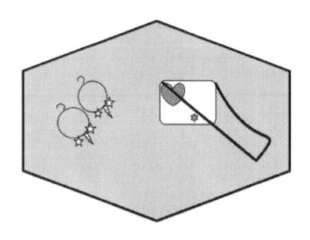

The Special Earrings

by

Hannah Royal

Have you ever wanted something so bad, you could see it every time you closed your eyes? Well, two girls, who were the exact opposites of each other did.

"Ugh! I need those earrings," Journey said out loud to her crazy, fun loving BFF, Magenta.

Magenta was quite frustrated with her vain, rebellious, and dramatic friend. "Yah, yah, I know. You want them so badly, they're burned into your eyelids. You've told me before."

Journey retorted, "You wouldn't understand. You're not very stylish."

Meanwhile, Candy, the adorable, girlish, diva, was doing the same thing to her friend Lyla, the shy, Japanese, bookworm. "I'm telling you Lyla, someone else probably has their eyes on them too." Candy explained.

"I doubt it, Candy," Lyla said quietly. "They are, $25. Except you, no one could be that in love with a pair of earrings." There were people around she didn't know.

"Whatever,"Candy said, indignantly.

The next day, at Wispy Woods Middle School, Magenta approached Journey who was leaning against her locker and reading a note.

"Hey Journey. Whatcha reading?" Magenta questioned.

Journey answered, "Oh it's just a note from John-John." Jonathon was Journey's 6th grade boyfriend, but They were in 7th grade.

"Ooh! What's it say?" Magenta asked, raising her eyebrows at Journey.

"Nothing," she replied.

"Oh, come on. It's got to be pretty juicy stuff, if you're not telling me — your best friend."

"Magenta!   Shut   up."   Journey lowered her voice. "People are staring."

"Oh,   let   them   stare."   Magenta mumbled, grabbing the note.

"Dear Journey," the note said. *"I saw you eyeing those earrings. Yah, they're a bit pricey, but you know it's almost your B-Day. Go to the cafeteria, and ask the lunch lady, "Where's the sparrow?" If she says she doesn't know, she's the wrong one. If she says, it's not on the grounds, she means — well, you're smart. You can figure it out. Once you've reached the destination, look for a huge rock. Turn it over, and you'll find directions to another secret*

location. There you will find your booty. Have fun on your treasure hunt. Love you.

Love,

John-John

"Oh, em, gee," Magenta shrieked, ."A treasure hunt from your boyfriend, for earrings. Awww, he's so sweet!"

"I know, right?" Journey jumped up and down. "He's so sweet to give such expensive earrings. I hope no one gets them before we do."

Meanwhile at Lyla's Grandma's

Candy stomped angrily back and forth. "Ugh! And <u>she</u> thinks she can buy my earrings? Umm — no."

"Shhh. Calm down, Candy," Lyla responded peacefully. "It'll be okay. You can just buy another pair."

"No, no I can't," Candy sobbed in response "That was the last pair!". "Plus the season is almost over, so no more of those same earrings will be ordered."

"Oh." Lyla looked down at her feet.

"Yah, not so fun," Candy said, matter-of-factly.

Inside the Cafeteria

"Yeah, uh, Hi Ms. Um, Marsh," Journey asked the bulging lunch lady. "Can you tell me where the sparrow is?"

"It's not on the grounds," Ms. Marsh said. "It's across the street."

"Okay," Magenta said, while she and Journey ran out of the building. "Thanks a bunch, Ms. Marsh. So do you have any idea where the rock is?" Magenta read

Jonathon's note over, and over, to see if it would give her any clues.

"I-D-K," Journey said, while she crawled on the ground searching for the biggest rock she could find. *WOHNK!* "Ouch that hurt!" Journey said, rubbing her head.

"Ha, ha, ha!" Magenta held her stomach and laughed so hard she couldn't breathe. "Did you just run into a rock?"

"Maybe," Journey said, still rubbing her head. "Hey! I think this is the rock!" Journey realized while she lifted the rock.

Magenta snatched the note from Journey's hand and read it. "Um, it says, *Go to his locker and wait.*"

Journey continued to rub her head. "Humph. All that pain, and for nothing!"

"Really? Your boyfriend is nutty," Magenta exclaimed.

When they all met up at Jonathon's locker, he pulled out a beautifully wrapped box, and handed it to Journey. "Here you go, sweetie," Jonathon said affectionately, "your precious earrings."

"Aww," Journey said sweetly as she took the box and opened it up.

"Thanks, babe."

"Ooh!" Magenta swooned when Journey pulled out the earrings and put them on.

"What do you think you're doing with my earrings?" Candy asked as she approached.

"What do you mean?" Journey said, confused while pointing to Jonathon.

"John-John bought them for me. They're not yours."

"Yah," Jonathon appeared confused. "I have no idea what you're talking about. I bought them with my money."

Candy steamed. "I had my eye on them first. I was even going to put them on hold, and then save up my money for them. But, <u>no,</u> you had to go and buy them for your stupid girlfriend!"

"You have <u>no</u> proof that <u>you</u> saw them first. What if I went to the store last month, and saw them, and showed them to, Journey? How do <u>you</u> know?"

Magenta said, "You have no right to accuse us of that, when you have zero proof."

After years of hate, and arguments, the girls finally made up. They compromised that they each get one earring, along with one earring of another pair they fought over.

So in conclusion — never love a pair of earrings, that a girl you particularly like, loves.

~THE END~

MY MORNING WISH

by

Christopher Chaffin

One morning I woke up and I made a wish that I knew what my dog was thinking. I put my clothes on and brushed my teeth. Then Princess, my dog, came in the bathroom. I leaned down to pet her, like I always do and said, "Good Morning Girl."

Then I walked into my room and she followed me like always. Anywhere I go, she goes. When I sat on my bed, she said "Good Morning Chris,"

I just sat there with my mouth open and didn't know what to say. Finally, I asked Princess some questions. "Who do you like better, me or my brother, Justin?"

Princess started wagging her tail, knocking everything down since she is a pit bull. Then she replied, "I like you both the same."

We went outside, and went for a walk, and I kept asking her questions. The neighbors started wondering who I was talking to. It didn't bother me at all, because I was just happy my dog could talk back to me.

We went back into the house to cool off and get some water. I watched T.V., and

Princess's puppies started crying. She went to the door. "Let me out," she said.

I let her out so she could take care of her puppies; I could hear her puppies saying, "Mama, come here."

I didn't know how it happened, and I thought it was a dream. I started pinching myself, and splashing water on my face, but Princess was still talking to me.

Finally, it was bedtime, and I put covers on the bed since it was cold. I petted Princess and told her goodnight.

"Goodnight Chris," she said.

The next morning, I woke up, put my clothes on, and brushed my teeth. Princess came in the bathroom again. I said, "Good morning Princess," but she didn't say anything.

Instead, she barked as usual. Princess went into the living room and sat by the door. The puppies were barking, and I let her outside to be with them. Because of my wish, I didn't have to wonder what they were saying anymore. Now I believe that wishes do come true.

~THE END~

You Are Beautiful On the Inside

by

Nellie Downie

Once upon a time, there were two rocks on an old road. One rock was beautiful. It had all the colors of a glorious sunset over the sea. It was smooth, perfectly round, and glittered like the dew on the grass in the morning sun.

The other rock was rather ugly. It was grey and rough. Dust had built up in its crevices, which just made it look worse. It was the ugliest rock on the road. Other rocks hated this rock, except the most beautiful rock. This rock saw her for what she truly was. On the outside, she saw an ugly rock, but on the inside, there was a stone more beautiful than herself.

The ugly rock was very kind, and loved her friend dearly. She was torn, because the other rocks hated her so much.

One day, the two rocks were by the side of the road, dodging the rude comments being thrown by the other rocks. "Don't listen to them," said the beautiful stone. "You're beautiful on the inside."

All of a sudden, the small, warm, hand of a toddler caressed the beautiful stone. The other hand threw the ugly rock onto the road.

Crack! The ugly stone split in half to reveal a glittering diamond.

"I told you!" exclaimed the beautiful stone. "You are beautiful on the inside!"

The toddler picked up the once ugly stone, brought it home, and placed it on a shelf with others like it. Over the years, she gathered more stones like this one. Under her collection, she placed a sign which read, "You're beautiful on the inside."

~THE END~

6th Grade 2012

Talk to the Hand

by

Rachel Nadeau

During the dog days of summer, I would see a young girl with disheveled hair walking past my house each afternoon. For some reason, she caught my attention. I would peek out of my bedroom window and anxiously wait for her each day. For weeks, I repeated this same ritual. Then one day, she stopped, turned slowly, and looked right at me. I quickly dropped to the floor, breathing heavily, as if I had just been caught. Slowly, I inched my way back up to my window. Ever so carefully, I pulled back the curtain, and slightly raised my eyes to see if she was gone.

The next day, I decided I would surprise her by hiding behind the tree in my front yard. I'd jump out as she passed by. As she approached, I crouched down, ready to spring out and surprise her. Then, I made my move.

"Hello," I said.

The girl simply kept strolling along; it didn't seem to faze her in the slightest way. I found this rather odd, so I followed along beside her. As we walked, she began to mumble something I couldn't comprehend. She began to do strange hand motions. Then, all of a sudden, it hit me—she must be deaf. That's why when I jumped out to scare her, she was not startled.

Not really understanding what she was saying, it was obvious she had a lot to say. The girl was making me laugh, as we walked along and laughed out loud.

Within minutes, it seemed we had arrived at her house. She grabbed my arm, and introduced me to her mother using sign language. Her mother told me her name was Sue, and her daughter's name was Linda. I asked her mom if she would teach me sign language, so Linda and I could talk. She agreed.

Each day, I would walk home with Linda, and learn more and more. Finally, I could understand her. Then, I could move my hands in strange ways without even realizing I was doing it. We became friends; lifelong friends. We understood each other in ways that were "unspeakable!"

~THE END~

6th Grade 2012

Friendship

by

Ryan Fitch

There I was, running through the woods far away from Asus. Asus is a bully. Earlier today, he told me that he was coming for me. Which means, his gang is with him. Luckily, my trusty friend Cooper, was beside me. He's like, a guy who knows wrestling moves, because all he watches is World Wrestling

Entertainment. So, he has my side in this fight.

Asus is gaining on us, so I turn and go for my house. Cooper knows what I'm doing, so he takes another turn. He's going around the block, to come in through my back door. I finally make it through the door of my house, and see Cooper standing there with a coke, and a Gatorade for me.

While we were inside, Asus and his gang stood in my yard taunting me; yelling, "Drake. You and Cooper are a bunch of wimps. Come out here and a fight like a man." Asus and his gang like to make fun of my name, even though Cooper and I can bench press more weight than they can.

It makes me wonder how good of a friend Cooper is. He always takes up for me, and I take up for him. That is just friendship. Cooper and I play my X-box for a little bit, then we go look outside. Asus and his gang are gone.

It's a cool day outside, and I decide to go outside to shoot hoops. Cooper and I play basketball on the seventh grade team. Cooper asks me if I want to play one-on-one. I say no, because Cooper is the best guard on the team. You just can't score a basket with him on you.

Today, Cooper and I have to go to school. We are straight A students. That means we're both in honors classes, which are easy for us, because we are supposed to be in these classes. So, we get to call each other, and help each other on homework.

But, we always get caught running our mouth at people, or teachers. So we are kind of airheads. We always kid each other, play around, and have fun—like the eating contest in the lunchroom. Cooper and I hold the record for the most chili dogs ate during lunch, which is six. I hold the milk chugging record of twelve cartons during lunch.

This is all about having a good friend and having fun. That's just one small step in having a great friendship. So, go out and find yourself a great friend to have fun with—a friend like me, and Cooper.

~THE END~

HALLOWEEN CUTIE

by

Taylor Anstee

I'm Miss Piggy, and I'm a pig. I love food. I live with four dogs; Puppy, Baxter, Little Cinny, and Cocoa. My favorite holiday is coming up—Halloween. I love Halloween because I get treats, and what's better than treats.

I'm not sure what I'm going to be for Halloween. I hope I decide quickly, because Halloween is three days away. My mommy said I have to go with Puppy.

Puppy asked, "What are you going to be?"

I said, "I'm not sure."

"I'm going to be a super dog," Puppy said.

"What should I be?" I asked.

"I don't know," Puppy said.

Tomorrow is Halloween and I know what I am going to be—a hotdog! After I get done trick or treating, I can eat it. My friend that lives with me, Taylor, will take me and Puppy trick or treating. I can't wait. Taylor is going to see if my costume fits, and it does.

Today is Halloween! I have my hotdog costume on, and Puppy has his on. Now, we're waiting on Taylor. I'm not sure what she is. I think she's a zombie. We're off to go trick or treating, and I'm ready.

We came to the first house. Taylor got some candy, then me, and next it's Puppy's turn.

I did a cute face, and Puppy did his tricks, but I can't do tricks. I can't even jump. Me and Puppy got lots of treats.

By the time it was ten o'clock, we went home. We looked at our treats, and Puppy had a whole basket full. There was nothing in mine. Then, I remembered, I ate it all. So, Puppy gave me some of his. I told him "thank you." I ate my treats and went to bed. That night, I realized I was wearing my hotdog costume.

~THE END~

6th Grade 2011

DON'T BLINK

by

Kaitlyn Biggar

"Mom. Please take me to the mall," Beth, my older sister, nagged.

"Fine," my mother insisted, "but just because you need some winter clothes. How about some new Uggs?"

Beth nodded her head in approval, and ran to the car.

My name is Lilly and I'm 12 years old. If you haven't noticed, my sister gets everything she wants! Beth is 14, going on 20, and she only cares about herself. Mom told me to come with them, so I jumped in the car, and we were off. I turned the Christmas music up really loud, and Beth screamed, "Lilly turn that junk off. No one cares about the holidays!"

Beth was wrong, because I absolutely adore Christmas. As we turned the corner, we saw a scary old man with a cardboard box that read: Please donate loose change. Beth looked at the sign and rolled her eyes, like she was so much better than everyone else.

I kept looking in his direction, and noticed a little girl. Actually, she was about my age. When I stared closer at the girl, I noticed that she was *more* than a random person off the street. She was my close friend, Addie. I rolled down the window and yelled her name.

Addie sprinted to our car and said, "I never wanted anyone to see me like this. Please give us a dollar, please."

My mother ripped open her purse, and handed Addie a $100 dollar bill. That was the money she was going to use to buy Beth's Uggs. Addie was so thankful; she gave my mom a big hug, and repeated the same words over and over. "Thank you."

Then, Addie and her father ran into McDonald's to get a hot meal.

Beth said, "Thank you for giving the Ugg money to her, Mom. She needed it more than I did."

That was strange. For that moment, Beth actually cared about someone other than herself, which was a massive deal. What I learned that day, and in that moment, was that any random person on the street could be your best friend. Or, they could be someone you saw walking in the hallway. Always be aware, and keep your eyes wide open. Don't blink, or you will miss the biggest opportunity of both your lives. So, maybe that was the best Christmas present ever. I'm glad I got to be a part of it, and realized the true meaning of giving.

~THE END~

7th Grade Stories

"You cannot depend on your eyes

when your imagination

is out of focus."

~Mark Twain

WARMTH

by

Blaire Berry

Fog. It overcrowded the windowpane and the atmosphere. I could barely make out the shapes of trees; then it started to downpour. The rain beat against the windowpane as though forcing itself into the boundaries of the house.

I sat, curled in a chair, staring as the sky wept. What else was there to do? I couldn't go outside, unless I wanted to get soaked; with the bonus of a cold. I could watch TV, except the power went out. Great. Because I didn't have a cell phone, my source of media entertainment was out. The only options were either reading, or working on that school project. But, I found staring out the window more amusing than the two combined.

Silence. A loud silence screamed at me, leaving me expecting something. Nothing happened. I was about to close my eyes. Dreams were more comforting and intriguing than my day, so far. That's when the silence was disturbed by a pounding on the front door.

When I was home alone, I wasn't supposed to open the door. But mentally, I'd reached my highest point of desperation.

I opened the door, shocked when something bounded past me, and into my house.

My friend Logyn, stood in the doorway. "Morning," she said plainly.

I stared, too confused to ask any questions.

"Can I come in?" she asked.

A bedraggled puppy bounced before us.

"I found it this morning," Logyn said, "and I've been trying to find its' owner. It needs some care, and I need your help."

I thought for a moment. "Yeah, I'm sorry, but…"

"Look," Logyn said, "I'm tired of your selfishness and laziness. You're going to help me, even if you disagree."

Dumbfounded, I waited for her to proceed.

"Well that was fun," Logyn said later, standing adjacent to me, and equally as drenched.

I might as well have been outside in the rain. The puppy on the other hand, was clean and dry, its' golden coat gleaming.

"We have to feed him. I brought some dog food," Logyn said.

I moaned internally.

By now, the puppy was well fed, clean, and looked healthy. The only problem was, I wasn't the owner, and had no desire to be. I was sure this was a complete waste of time, until someone knocked on the door.

We opened the door, and the puppy bounded into the arms of a teenage girl. "I've been looking for you for days. Were you two taking care of him?" she asked.

We nodded.

"Thank you so much. I can't tell you how grateful I am." She was elated, and I had to smile.

In that moment, I realized what Logyn meant about me. I was selfish, and lazy. From then on, I decided that giving was far more important than receiving. Because, when you give, you receive a feeling of warmth. My day was now filled with sunshine.

~THE END~

7th Grade 2012

The Griffin's Hunter

by

Elizabeth Stone

Once upon a time, there was a girl who hunted magick. That girl was my sister, and I'm here to tell her story, or rather one of them. The last time she tried, I had just turned twelve. It was the day before and my sister would be twenty, in two weeks. She was going on another hunt, and I wanted to follow. "Please. Oh, please, Sarah. Let me come."

"No. It's way too dangerous."

"Oh Sarah, we both know you've never found anything." She shot me a look. This subject was forbidden and I knew it. "Please, Sarah? I really wanna go."

"I'll think about it. Go get ready."

"You've been bossy ever since Mum and Dad died in the Amazon, last year!"

"I feel responsible for you, kid. Get ready."

"Fine!" I ran up the stairs, and was ready quickly.

School went by in a blur. Before I knew it, I was busting into the parlor where Sarah sat with several bags.

"Wow," I said. "Where you headed? Space?"

"No. You're coming with me."

"Really?"

"Yes."

"Oh, Sarah! Thank you so much!"

She laughed. "No problem, kiddo."

As we boarded the plane to Alaska, Sarah told me what we were looking for. "A griffin. It's a half-lion, half-eagle creature, and there have been sightings in the mountains."

"Sounds fun."

Sarah seemed so happy, even though I was being sarcastic. "Doesn't it though? I've already mapped and charted our route up the mountain."

"I'm sure it'll be awesome."

When we stepped off the plane, Sarah dragged me to a cab. "Mountain Rescued Cabins please."

The driver sped toward our destination. Coming up the road, I could see in the dense wood, a pack of wolves on the hunt. They kept pace for a while before breaking away, leaving me to stare at nothing. I sighed as we pulled up. Sarah dragged me down a trail.

"A Cabin?" I said.

"Oh no. We sleep in tents. Come on."

The first excruciating five days went by with little event. Then, in the distance we heard a roar. The creature landed so close Sarah.

"Jenny," she whispered softly to me, "run!"

"What about you?"

"I have to take care of you." Sarah produced a weapon.

"But, Sarah!"

"I said run! Go!" I could barely see as I dived for a small cave. Tears of fear for my sister's life made it hard to see. I never knew how much she, or I, loved each other until that night. It seemed the battle went on forever before the griffin won, and flew away.

Afterwards, I was in the cabin's lobby, telling the attendant about my sister. The attendant rushed me to a room, and then sent up some warm food. Soon, she adopted me and we lived out the remainder of her life together.

Now you know the tale, and I must leave. I mean, someone must carry on my sister's legacy. And face it, that person is me. Jenny Renae Reckends, Magick Hunter of 2012.

~THE END~

Courage

by

Kaitlyn Biggar

"Kaitlyn," my teacher announced, "it's your turn to present your project on someone who inspires you."

As I opened my mouth to speak, I saw my best friend, Sara. She had tears in her eyes, because she knew what I was going to say.

"In 2004, Billie Lee Davis was diagnosed with ALS, a disease that attacks the muscle system. She struggled with losing the ability to walk, feed herself, and all the things we take for granted. Although she struggled with these everyday things, she never once complained."

My eyes filled with foggy tears, but Sara nodded at me in reassurance, so I could finish the story. As my voice cracked, I started again. "Billie was a very brave woman. She always stood strong in what she believed in. She was an amazing Christian. My goal in life is to be like her, not in the sense of not being able to walk, but to be as grateful as she was."

I finished the presentation with a sigh of relief. Pressure came upon me when student's hands went flying in the air. "Pick me! Pick me!" all the students yelled. Then, I pointed to a boy that was almost falling out of his chair. He wanted to be picked so badly.

"Why didn't you pick someone famous like Justin Bieber, or something?"

I laughed. I think everyone did. "You don't have to be famous to be an inspiration to someone," I answered in a calm tone.

The next hand raised was one of my other friends, Claire. She had the biggest grin on her face. "Has she passed away yet, or is she still living?"

I took a breath before answering. "She passed away September 19, 2010."

Strangely enough, Sara's hand was raised, so I picked her.

"How did you know her?"

I was so confused; I thought she knew the answer to this question already.

"She was my grandmother — Grammy. She lived with me for three years, and I helped take care of her until she died. She is the biggest inspiration to me. How did you not know that?"

The classroom became cold with silence.

Sara stated, "I knew the answer, but you just overcame your fear of telling people how you feel. You can do more than what you think."

I dropped my jaw in amazement over what I just shared with my classmates.

My inspiration, and I didn't even stutter. "I see what you did there," I whispered to Sara after class. "You're my inspiration too, and thanks for always believing in me."

~THE END~

The Big Day!

by

Kassi Holder

When I was born, they took me from my mom, because of her conditions. I was in a foster home for 3 months. My dad's mom and her husband came to the foster home and took me home with them. Then, I didn't know who they were, but they knew who I was. The only reason they knew me, was because my mom had called them. They have had me for 12 years, and I am living at the house I was meant to be at.

My new parents are Butch and Kennetta Holder. They legally adopted me when I was 7 years old. I can remember that day, like it was yesterday. We were just sitting in a courtroom listening to a judge talk to Kennetta. Since I could talk, I called her Nana, and I called Butch, Papa.

I know I'm here for a reason, and a good reason. So, I wouldn't change a thing. I still talk to my mom, and I get to see my dad a lot because he lives in town. My mom lives in Florida with my two sisters and brother. I know I'm loved. If my papa and nana didn't adopt me, who knows where I would be now. I know I am a lucky girl. I wouldn't change the big day we received papers saying that, Kassi Coley, now belongs to Butch and Kennetta Holder.

I am proud to have the name, Kassi Holder.

~THE END~

8th Grade

Stories

"Our truest life is when we are in dreams awake."

Henry David Thoreau

8th Grade 2012

Searching For The Silver Lining

by

Graci Runk

I'll never forget that devastating day, I found out one of my best friends, Mason, had Leukemia. It truly sickened me to know that a good person like him would have to face the struggle of cancer at such a young age. I knew that Mason could pull through, but this battle was going to be very tough on just a little fourth grade boy.

It all started in October of 2008. Mason and I were sitting at the lunch table, when he started talking about having a cold.

"Graci, do you think I have a fever?" Mason asked.

As I felt his forehead, I knew something wasn't right. "Mason, I think you need to go to the nurse," I replied.

After lunch, I noticed that Mason had gone home. I assumed it was because of his cold. If only I knew, that this would be the start of Mason's difficult journey.

Mason was absent from school for around a week before Mrs. Terry, our teacher, announced that Mason had cancer.

She assured us that the Leukemia was curable, but Mason would be absent for most of the year. I pondered about Mason's cancer, and I couldn't believe that God would allow such an awful thing happen to such a great friend.

A few months went by, and Mason gradually got better. He celebrated his tenth birthday on December 2nd, and finally he returned to school in January. He got to see his friends a lot more because his immune system was building up. We always had to be extra careful, because even a small sneeze could send him over the edge

However, Mason's liver started to fail, and he died on March 28, 2009. The following morning, my mother told me the bad news. Mason's death has heavily affected me in many ways. The months after Mason died were tough on me and my classmates. Some days, I couldn't get myself out of bed. I couldn't face the fact that Mason was gone. This was the lowest point in my life, and I felt like I was all alone.

As I graduated from the fourth grade, I finally got on my feet. I started having friends over again, and I began to find myself smiling more. Since the fourth grade, I have come a long way. Soon, I started to realize I couldn't grieve over the time I didn't spend with Mason, but I could be grateful for the ten years I did have with him. I began to pray to God, and thank him for putting Mason in my life, and giving me such a wonderful friend.

Even though I lost Mason in the fourth grade, I don't regret anything that happened. This whole situation has shaped me into the person I am today, and it has put me closer to God. I know that Mason is an angel looking down on me, and he protects me.

~THE END~

8th Grade 2012

FRIEND OR ENEMY

by

Haley Thompson

My name is Haley Thompson. When most people think of a family, they think of a white picket fence, a happy married couple grilling hamburgers and hotdogs in their backyard, children playing, and a dog playing with them.

Well, my family is sort of like that. We have no white picket fence, but my parents are happily married, and have been for sixteen years. They have us, of course, and we had a dog named Daisy. What started out to be getting a puppy when we were four, turned us into being a closer family. Daisy made us laugh with the crazy things she did.

Around two or three years ago, up walked a thin, scraggly looking cat. She didn't have a collar or anything. Well, she was scared of us at first. We called her up to us by making cat sounds. "Meow. Meow. Meow. Meow." We kept repeating that, and she finally walked up to us.

We fed her a can of Ol'Roy wet dog food. She gulped it down like that was the last meal she was going to get. Well, Daisy was in the house at the time. Since the word, *meow* was the only thing she responded too, we just started calling her, Meow-Meow.

The new chapter of her life began. Everything with her had to go slow. It was a while before she would even let us touch her. She slowly began to grow. Every day she would show up, and wait for us to feed her. Some days, when she wasn't there, we would call her name, and she would come running. That went on for about a year and a half.

Then one day, she actually let us love on her. She was so sweet. Each day, she would let us love on her, but she was real skittish as all cats are. One really pretty day, dad brought her inside the house. She stayed in that one spot for a while, as if to say, "What am I supposed to do?"

We kept telling her she could walk around. Then, she kind of inched around the house a little bit, smelling everything. We sat on the floor and let her walk up to us and love on us. Of course, Daisy was outside.

Daisy was already six years old, so when dad brought Meow-Meow in, Daisy went out. Then, after a while, daisy wanted back in. Dad took Meow-Meow to the back door, and let her out that way, while Daisy came in the front door.

Immediately, Daisy smelled everywhere the cat had been. A few short months later, the cat was finally letting us pick her up. Those were some fun times. Whenever she got scared, she would leap out of our arms. A little while after that, Meow-Meow jumped over Daisy's fence and started whining, because she wanted inside. It almost sounded like she was hollering, "Hey you guys. Will you let me in?" Well, when we opened the door, Daisy shot out and trapped the cat under the bench. She was sitting back on her paws like she was ready to hit Daisy in the face.

Meow-Meow was saying, "If you don't get away from me, dog, you'll have scratches on your nose!"

Daisy said, "Whatever cat. This is my territory; my house!" Right about that time, Daisy stuck her muzzle under that bench, and Meow-Meow scratched her nose.

Meow-Meow shot out from under that bench, and leaped over the fence. Meow-Meow was like, "Ha, ha. I told you dog."

Meow-Meow learned that day, to never cross that fence again. But the truth is, even if you don't know somebody, you never know if you'll be their friend, or enemy. Maybe you'll see your pets talking to each other.

~THE END~

LOST AND FOUND

by

Kayleigh McDonald

Carly looked over her shoulder repeatedly, feeling like someone was watching her. All she saw was an old man walking in the opposite direction, and a girl sitting on a bench absorbed in a book. Carly kept on walking, jumping at every sound she heard. One last look, and Carly saw a little girl walking behind her.

The girl was dressed in a thin summer dress and sandals. Her teddy bear was being drag behind her. Her face was tear-stained, and a lost expression was imprinted on her face. Carly decided to do the right thing, and help the girl.

"What's wrong?" Carly asked, kneeling down in front of her.

"I lost my mommy," she said, pouting and sniffing.

"Where did you last see her?" Carly asked.

"At the park," she told Carly. "She went to the bathroom and never came back. I waited a long time."

Carly smiled. "I'll help you find her."

"Mommy told me don't talk to strangers," the little girl replied.

"It's all right, you can trust me." Carly held out her hand. The little girl took it. "What is your name?"

"Brianne."

"Mine is Carly."

They walked hand in hand to the park. Half way down the second block, an ice cream truck drove by. Brianne jumped up and down excitedly pointing at the truck.

They walked over and then ordered a Sponge Bob Popsicle. The little girl took Carly's hand and happily licked the Popsicle. They headed to the park once again.

As they walked the next two blocks Carly asked Brianne what grade she was in, and many other things.

When they arrived at the park, they searched for Brianne's mom. They walked all over the track, until they heard somebody calling a name. It sounded like a young woman's voice.

"That sounds like Mommy!" Brianne jumped up and down.

"Come on, let's find her."

Carly led the little girl to the voice. They walked over a hill and saw a woman in her mid to late twenties. Her blonde hair looked like it was brushed through many times by her hands, and her posture showed her worry.

"Mommy!" Brianne yelled, running to the woman.

The woman spun around, and relief filled her face. Her blue eyes twinkled.

"Brianne!" she exclaimed, holding out her arms.

The 6-year-old girl sprinted and jumped into the young woman's arms.

Carly saw Brianne pointing at her, then her mother waved, and motioned her to come over where they stood. Carly walked over and smiled.

Brianne's mother thanked her. "Thank you for watching her."

"It's no problem." Carly smiled happily.

"I was wondering if you can baby-sit Brianne sometimes, since you took such good care for her. Call me Julie, by the way." Julie smiled.

"I'd be delighted, but I need to go."
Carly smiled, feeling good. "Bye, thanks
again." She smiled while waving

"Bye Carly!" Brianne smiled.

~THE END~

FIND THE CHILD IN YOU

By

Tammy D. Thompson

Dig deep and close your eyes

Going back to a time gone away,

But still you can remember

Just like yesterday.

Remember your wishes, dreams and wants,

And the friends you held so dear.

Remember all the things you wanted to do

And the things you used to fear.

Reach inside and embrace that child

And find the peace within,

For no matter how old you are

That child is still your friend.

Find the innocence that once consumed you

Where hope wasn't far away.

Remember then, like you remember now

For it was only yesterday.

Dig deep and close your eyes

Then smile as you embrace

The one that you used to be

And remember that youngsters face.

Find the child that's in you

With the dreams you held onto.

Reach once more for those dreams

Then maybe they'll come true.

Find The Child In You!

Aspiring Authors Listed Alphabetically

Taylor Anstee

Garrett Bennett

Blaire Berry

Kaitlyn Biggar

Christopher Chaffin

Justin Chaffin

Nellie Downie

Ryan Fitch

Judah *'Zack'* Franklin

Abigail George

Shay N. Gibson

Brianna Hall

Kassi Holder

Charli Hueter

Johnni Hueter

Camille Janes

Kayleigh McDonald

Adeline L. Moss

Maelyn Moss

Rachel Nadeau

Layla Nowlin

Bailey Paschal

Elaina Robertson

Aliyah Royal

Hannah Royal

Graci Runk

Kayla Shew

Elizabeth Stone

Haley Thompson

Kasey Whittington

Dear Reader,

It has been our pleasure to undertake such a worthy venture. Each story has touched our hearts in some way. It is our prayer, that St. Jude Children's Research Hospital benefits greatly from this endeavor. Your proceeds and donations, will make a difference in the life of a child. After all, we are all an extension of God's wonderful hand.

Topaz Publishing, Publisher, Sr. Editor, & Staff October 9, 2012